READY RABBIT?

Fiona Roberton

Rabbit?

Rabbit, are you
in there?

Rabbit, why
are you **hiding?**

I am **not** hiding.

Ah. Well, you need to **get ready,** Rabbit.

It's time to go to the party.

Well...

...maybe.

What's wrong,
Rabbit?

I don't want to
go to the party.

But why, Rabbit? You will have a **lovely** time, I promise.

All of your friends will be there.

Really? Will Hugo be there?

Yes!

And Charlie and Anna and Thomas and Frank?

Yes, **everyone** will be there.

WHAT if it's too LOUD?
And what if there's a
OR some OTHER
And what if I get tired?
AND what if MARCUS
And what if I fall over?

OUCH!

Parties can be VERY NOISY.

SPIDER in the bathroom?

STRANGE creature?

and want to come home?

is there? Marcus is mean.

and HURT myself?

And what if...?

Don't worry, Rabbit. There will be lots of **fun things** at the party.

There will be **music** and **dancing** and **cake.**

and
BALLOONS
and
PRESENTS
and
CARROTS.

And
GAMES
and
PRIZES

Yes,
CAKE!

I know you do, Rabbit.
And you can wear
whatever you like.

You can even wear that **lovely**
jumper Grandma gave you.

Of course! You look **AMAZING,** Rabbit.

Thank you.

So, are you **ready, Rabbit?**

I think so.

Excellent.
Then shall we?

Ah. Well, everybody's out here dancing.
I LOVE dancing.
I know you do. So, don't you want to come and dance with me?
Um, Maybe.
OK.

For Eirin, who never says no to a party.

HODDER CHILDREN'S BOOKS
First published in Great Britain in 2019 by Hodder Children's Books.

A CIP catalogue record for this book is available from the British Library.

HB ISBN: 978 1 444 93727 5
PB ISBN: 978 1 444 93728 2

1 3 5 7 9 10 8 6 4 2

Printed and bound in China

Hodder Children's Books, an imprint of Hachette Children's Group, part of Hodder and Stoughton,
Carmelite House, 50 Victoria Embankment, London, EC4Y 0DZ

An Hachette UK Company
www.hachette.co.uk
www.hachettechildrens.co.uk

Hodder
Children's
Books